DANIEL NESQUENS

MIREN ASIAIN LORA

A GOOD DAY

The cat and the tiger were the best of friends.

They were always together—

the tiger with his striped coat and the cat

with his little hat and his sweater decorated with mice.

The tiger inside his cage, and the cat outside.

Or sometimes inside.

The cat told the tiger things he had never told anyone else.

"I really like that cat walking by the toucan cage."

And "that monkey is hateful."

The tiger listened very well.

The cat was very punctual—and the tiger even more so.

"Tomorrow, at eleven minutes past ten, you'll see me at the gate," the cat said.

"I'll have a big slice of cake in one paw, and an umbrella in the other."

"Is it going to rain?" the tiger asked.

"I don't know, but just in case."

"You know," the cat said to the tiger, "sometimes
I wish I were like you—big, smart, strong . . . "

"And I wish I were like you," said the tiger.

"Really? Why? I'm weak and tiny . . . "

"And free."

"Well, yes. That's true."

The cat and the tiger were the best of friends.

They spent a great deal of time together.

There were even some nights when the cat slept at the zoo.

"Tell me, how many stars do you see?" the tiger asked.

"More than I can count. When I get to a hundred and something,
I lose track."

"What I liked most about being free was watching the moon
and the stars shining on the river," the tiger said.

"More than chasing gazelles?"

"Much more. One night, I was quietly drinking,
and I saw a crocodile open his mouth . . . "

"And?"

"And he ate the moon!"

"Oh, come on."

The tiger did love to exaggerate a bit.
But it made the cat sad that his friend
was always talking about not being free.
"Where will you feel better than
you do here?" he asked.

"Home," the tiger answered.

"Help me escape. Help me get away from here.
I can't stand this anymore," the tiger said one day.

"I don't know how," the cat said. "If I were a magician,
I could make you disappear. Or if I were very strong,
I could break the bars. Or . . . "

"It's much simpler than that.
Listen . . ." the tiger said.

"Did you understand all of that?" the tiger
asked nervously, once he had finished.

"Perfectly," the cat replied.

"Do you have any questions?"

"What are you going to do once you're free?"

"I'll go back home."

"You'll have to cross borders."

"I will."

"You'll have to cross the ocean."

"I will."

"You'll have to walk through deserts."

"I will."

The cat and the tiger were the best of friends.

And the cat was very punctual.

That night, he didn't need his little hat—just a bit of luck.

The keys were right there for anyone to see.

But . . .

"Where do you think you're going with those keys?"

the zookeeper asked sternly.

The cat lost one of his lives.

"I'm going to free my friend, the tiger.
He misses his home,
the wind on his face, the tree branches,
the smell of jasmine, the stars in the sky,
the moon shining on the river,
the antelopes running . . . "

"Okay," the zookeeper said.
"But don't tell anyone. This is our secret."
The cat nodded.

SECURITY

The cat and the zookeeper became the best of friends.

Every night you would see them together, smiling and laughing.

The keeper told the cat things he had never told anyone else.

"I'm in love. Her name is Anna. Her eyes . . . oh, her eyes . . ."

Or "I received a letter from our friend the tiger.

He's already counted five thousand two hundred and fifty stars.

When he gets to a million, he's going to throw a party."

"When I get to a hundred and something, I lose track,"
the cat said, and lowered his hat over his ears.

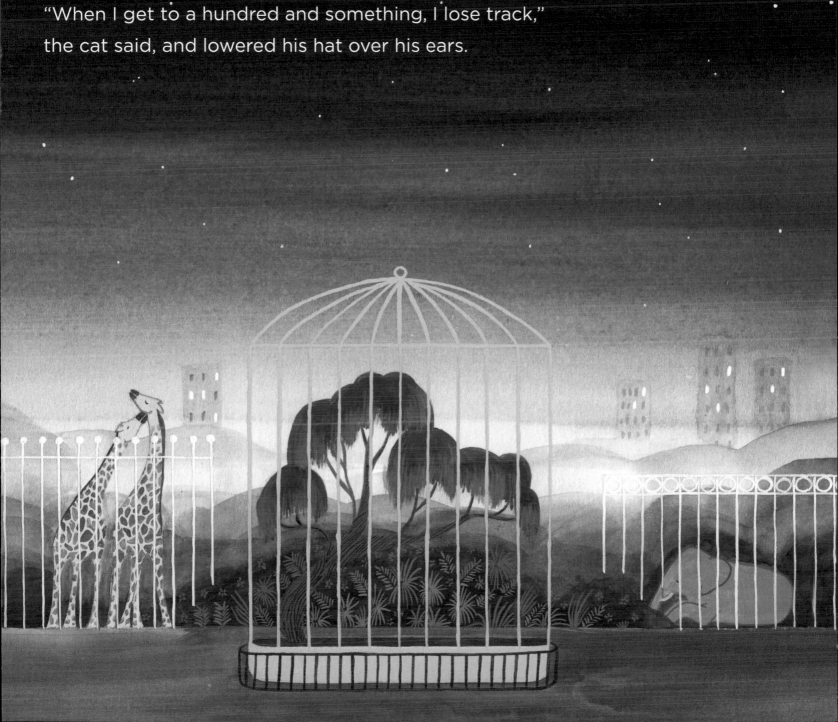

Daniel Nesquens has been writing children's books for over ten years. He has published more than thirty titles, including *Mister H* (Eerdmans) and *My Tattooed Dad* (Groundwood). He loves infusing his stories with humor and magical realism. Daniel lives in Spain.

Miren Asiain Lora grew up in Spain, where she studied fine arts at the University of the Basque Country. Her artwork has been shown in exhibitions in Spain, Argentina, Italy, and Mexico. In her illustrations, Miren works to convey the magic of everyday life. She lives in Buenos Aires. Visit her website at www.miaslo.com.

First published in the United States in 2019
by Eerdmans Books for Young Readers,
an imprint of Wm. B. Eerdmans Publishing Co.
Grand Rapids, Michigan

www.eerdmans.com/youngreaders

Originally published in Spain under the title *Un buen día*
Text © Daniel Nesquens, 2017
Illustrations © Miren Asiain Lora, 2017
Published in agreement with Phileas Fogg Agency
www.phileasfoggagency.com
English-language translation © Eerdmans Books for Young Readers.

Manufactured in China

27 26 25 24 23 22 21 20 19   1 2 3 4 5 6 7 8 9

ISBN 978-0-8028-5530-5

A catalog record of this book is available from the Library of Congress.